School of Fish

Testing the Waters

By Jane Yolen

Illustrated by Mike Moran

Ready-to-Read

Simon Spotlight
New York London Toronto Sydney New Delhi

SIMON SPOTLIGHT
An imprint of Simon & Schuster Children's Publishing Division
1230 Avenue of the Americas, New York, New York 10020
This Simon Spotlight edition August 2020

For information about special discounts for bulk purchases, please contact
Simon & Schuster Special Sales at 1-866-506-1949 or business@simonandschuster.com.
Manufactured in the United States of America 0720 LAK
10 9 8 7 6 5 4 3 2 1
Names: Yolen, Jane, 1939– author. | Moran, Mike, 1957– illustrator.
Title: Testing the waters / by Jane Yolen ; illustrated by Mike Moran.
Description: Simon Spotlight edition. | New York : Simon Spotlight, 2020.
Series: School of fish | Summary: "A fish is nervous about a test and a mean-looking substitute teacher at school"—Provided by publisher.
Identifiers: LCCN 2020012088 (print) | LCCN 2020012089 (eBook)
ISBN 9781534466258 (paperback) | ISBN 9781534466265 (hardcover)
ISBN 9781534466272 (eBook)
Subjects: CYAC: Stories in rhyme. | Examinations—Fiction. | Test anxiety—Fiction.
Teachers—Fiction. | Schools—Fiction. | Fishes—Fiction.
Classification: LCC PZ8.3.Y76 Tes 2020 (print) | LCC PZ8.3.Y76 (eBook)
DDC [E]—dc23
LC record available at https://lccn.loc.gov/2020012088
LC eBook record available at https://lccn.loc.gov/2020012089

I'm silver. I'm cool.

I'm off to school.

My lunch box is packed.

My pencils are stacked.

It's swim test today.
My tummy is whirling
just like two currents,
angry and swirling.

None of my swim studies
stick in my head.
Going to school today
fills me with dread.

The shark bus comes
right after dawn.
I grab my pack.
Then I get on.

Silence today
feels like the rule.
No one seems sleek,
and no one is cool.

One tuna mentions
the scary swim test.
Some bubble and sigh.
Groans from the rest.

"Close your eyes tightly," I tell them, "and then take a deep breath and count to ten."

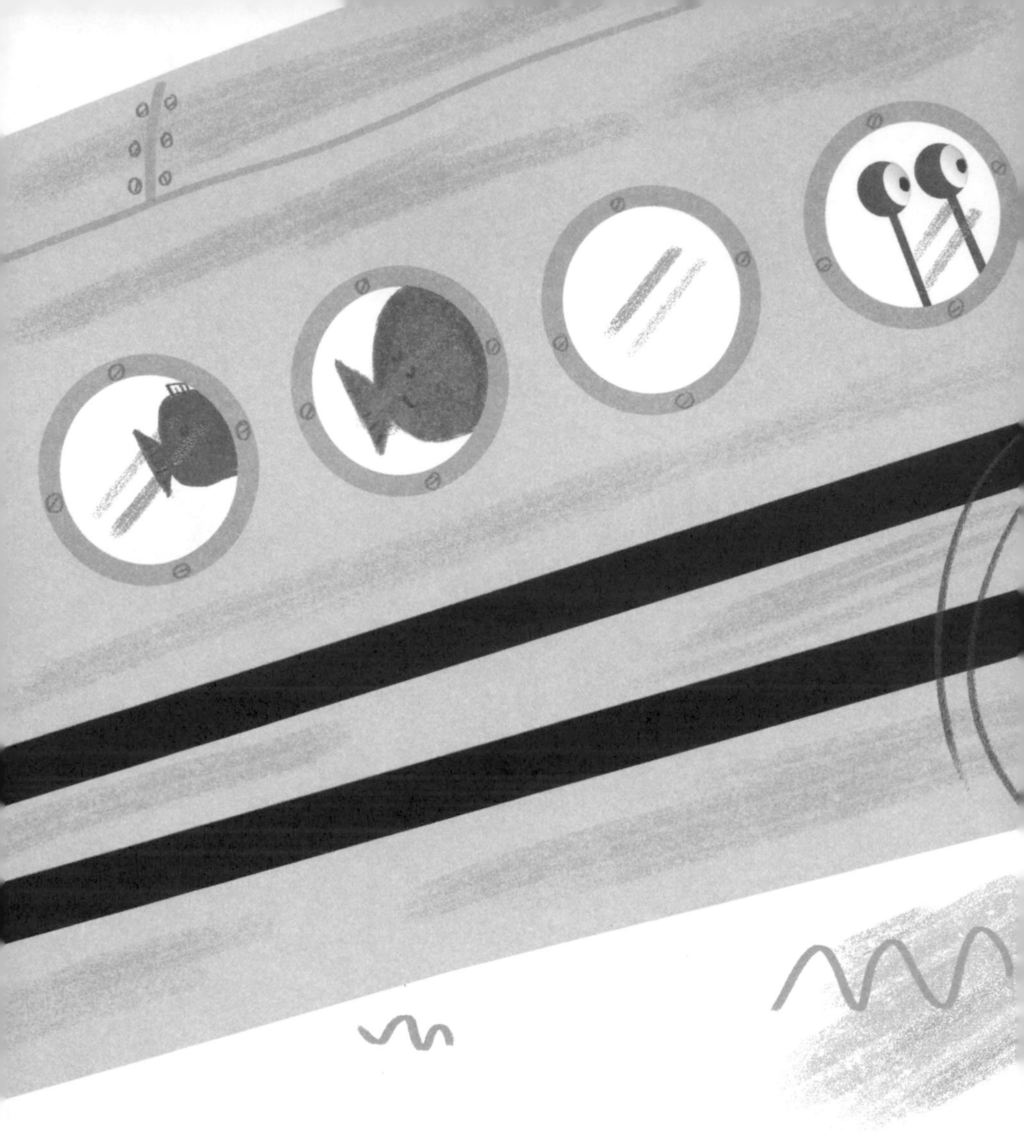

The count calms us all.
We arrive at our school.
We're all really sleek,
and we're all sort of cool.

Then a new swim coach,
with a real mean look,
says, "You can call me
Captain Snook."

His pointed teeth
and staring eyes
do not make this
a good surprise.

Snook passes out
the tests to all.

I glance around

the silent hall.

I look about

for my best friend.

I try my hardest

to pretend

that I am cool.

But I can see
that she is
just as scared as me.

“Begin!” growls Snook
and leaves the room.
We all prepare to
meet our doom.

I can't remember
fin from tail,
or who swims faster:
shark or whale?

My tears fall slowly,

turn to salt.

I'll fail the test.

It's all Snook's fault.

But I made myself
count up to ten,
look at the test,
and start again. . . .

And then . . .

I know the answers:

fin from tail.

And who swims faster:

NOT a whale!

The door creaks open—

in swims Snook.

This time he gives
a real nice look.

Then Snook says,
“You all were scared!
But I bet
all of you prepared.
So A’s all round.
You passed the test.”

I take a deep breath
and so do the rest.

“This lesson,” Snook says,

“was to stay calm

and swim forward—

never back.

Now it’s time

for games and snack.”

I shout out to Snook
and to our class,
“Captain, we give you
a great BIG pass!
You are silver
through and through!”

A
A
A
A
A
A
A
A

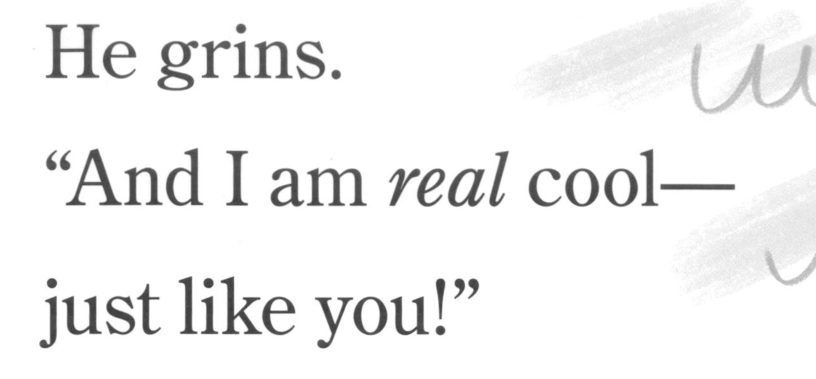

He grins.
“And I am *real* cool—
—just like you!”